THE DUCK WHO DIDN'T LIKE WATER

STEVE SMALL

SIMON & SCHUSTER
London   New York   Sydney   Toronto   New Delhi

For Monica

SIMON & SCHUSTER
First published in Great Britain in 2021 by Simon & Schuster UK Ltd
1st Floor, 222 Gray's Inn Road, London WC1X 8HB
This paperback edition published in 2022

A CIP catalogue record for this book is available from
the British Library upon request

ISBN: 978-1-4711-9234-0 (HB)
ISBN: 978-1-4711-9235-7 (PB)
ISBN: 978-1-4711-9236-4 (eBook)

Printed in China
1 3 5 7 9 10 8 6 4 2

There was once a duck
who didn't like water.

Duck didn't like swimming in it . . .

or paddling in it.

PLOP!

And Duck didn't like it
when it rained.

PLIP!

Not even if it rained just a little bit.

PLOP!

On rainy days, Duck liked nothing more
than curling up with a good book and
a hot drink.

I don't need to go outside,
Duck thought. *I've got*
everything I need right here.

And mostly that was true.

SIGH

One very windy and rainy night,
Duck was woken up by a loud noise . . .

and discovered a hole in the roof.

Well, I can't fix that tonight, Duck thought.

So Duck popped outside for a bucket . . .

and found an unexpected visitor,
who was lost. Very lost.

"Why don't you rest here for the night
where it's warm and dry?" asked Duck.

Frog cheerfully agreed, even though Frog
liked water **very** much.

The next morning, Duck said,
"We need to get you home,
but first we need to find out
where home actually is."

"OK," said Frog.

RIBBIT

So off they went.

They searched
EVERYWHERE . . .

but they couldn't find
Frog's home,

so they stopped for some lunch.

They set off again, but no
matter who they asked,

or where they looked,

they STILL couldn't find Frog's home.

So that night they ate dinner,
read each other stories,

said goodnight

G'NIGHT

and went to bed.

RIBBIT

The next morning, Pelican dropped by.
"Hello, Frog. You're a long way from home."

"Wait!" said Duck. "Do you know where
Frog lives?"

"Sure! It's all the way over in the next
river," Pelican replied. "Need a lift?"

By way of a goodbye, Duck gave Frog
two gifts: a good book and
a small umbrella.

Frog said a BIG
thank you.

RIBBIT

And moments later, Frog was gone.

Days went by. Everything was
the same as before.

But it felt different.

Something
was missing.

PLIK!

PLIK!

So Duck
set off.

And though it rained and it poured . . .

and the wind blew this way . . .

and that,

Duck did not give up.

Until, quite suddenly . . .

. . . Duck found Frog!

"Home doesn't feel like home
if you're not there!" Duck said.

And Frog agreed.

So Duck and Frog returned to their
old routines. They visited their new friends,

read stories to each other and,

perhaps most importantly of all . . .

. . . they fixed the hole in the roof.